Still *More* TWO-MINUTE MYSTERIES

Donald J. Sobol

AN
APPLE®
PAPERBACK

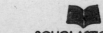

SCHOLASTIC INC.
New York Toronto London Auckland Sydney

For Kaethe Spiegel

Other books by the author
available from Scholastic Inc.:

Two-Minute Mysteries
More Two-Minute Mysteries
Encyclopedia Brown Carries On
Encyclopedia Brown and the Case of the
   Dead Eagles
Encyclopedia Brown Sets the Pace
Encyclopedia Brown and the Case of the
   Exploding Plumbing
Encyclopedia Brown Solves Them All

ISBN 0-590-41137-3

Copyright © 1975 by Donald J. Sobol. All rights reserved. Published by Scholastic Inc.

12 11 10 9 8 7 6 5 4 3 2 1   7 8 9/8 0 1/9

Printed in the U.S.A.   01

The Case of
the Arctic Explorer

Sir James Harvey, aged bachelor and famed explorer of the North Pole, was found murdered in his bedroom.

The $400,000 in thousand-dollar bills, which he was known to keep in his wall safe, was missing.

The police concluded that the criminal or criminals had concealed the money in the house, perhaps in something brought along for the purpose, expecting to recover it later.

This surmise was founded upon Sir James's eccentric precautions. A visitor might gain admission to his estate unchallenged. But no one, including the servants, could leave without being challenged by a series of private guards.

On the day Sir James's possessions were put on auction, Dr. Haledjian joined Sheriff Monahan in the explorer's museum.

"The sale starts in here," said the sheriff. "But every stick in the house will be sold today or tomorrow."

An auctioneer had begun to enumerate for the crowd of buyers the museum's objects, describing them as Sir James's favorite momentos of his five trips to the Arctic.

The objects included a group of stuffed animals — two polar bears and a penguin — three stuffed fish, and an assortment of Eskimo clothing, utensils, and weapons.

"The murderer has to be in the house," said the sheriff. "But my men can't watch all the rooms."

"Rest at ease," said Haledjian. "He or an accomplice is in this room, ready to make a purchase."

HOW DID HALEDJIAN KNOW?

Solution

Haledjian realized the criminal had hidden the money in his own prop—the one thing in the museum which didn't belong with a collection of North Pole objects. The stuffed penguin. The criminal forgot that penguins live in the South, not the North, Pole!

The Case of
the Arrowless Bow

The chief clue in the death of Bart Weaver was an archery bow, lying on the carpet at the top of a narrow twisting flight of stairs in his home.

"Weaver was found at the bottom of the stairs, his neck broken," Inspector Winters told Dr. Haledjian. "Had he fallen, his momentum would not have carried him around the twists in the stairs. He was pushed, and hard.

"As far as we can determine, the only thing missing from the house is Weaver's famous Luzon diamond. My theory is that Weaver heard burglars. Fearing for the diamond, he tied it to an arrow and shot it out this open window, expecting to reclaim it later."

"An exotic theory, but perhaps true," said Haledjian.

"Our prime suspect is Hugh Tiff. He's been trying to buy the diamond for years," said the inspector. "I'm having him picked up."

Haledjian hid the bow. The two men descended the stairs just as Tiff was brought in by two policemen.

Tiff listened arrogantly as the inspector said, "Bart Weaver was pushed down these stairs and killed. The Luzon diamond is missing. Were you in this house during the past three hours?"

"No, and I don't know a thing about Weaver's

death," insisted Tiff. "But find the diamond, you dumb cop! I'll buy it!"

"The diamond won't be hard to locate," said Haledjian. And staring up at the top of the narrow staircase, he added, "It's only an arrow flight away."

"Then let's go outside and look!" exclaimed Tiff.

"Arrest him," snapped Haledjian.

HOW COME?

Solution

As Haledjian stared at the stairs, Tiff, had he really known nothing, would have heard the sleuth say, ". . . a narrow flight away," not ". . . an arrow flight away."

Tiff should have said to look for the diamonds upstairs, not "outside."

The Case of
the Barbecue Murder

"Bill would have met your train himself, Dr. Haledjian," said Nora Perkins. "But since I was in town, he asked me to pick you up. He wanted more time to prepare the barbecue."

Bill Perkins, however, was past worrying about barbecues when Haledjian and his hostess arrived at the house half an hour later. Nora shrieked. Her husband lay on the lawn, a knife protruding from his chest.

A hasty examination indicated to Haledjian that the killing had occurred about an hour before. He studied the scene.

A half-cooked steak lay above flameless coals banked in a stone barbecue pit. Upon an iron shelf were a tray of condiments and a long-handled knife and fork.

"Who are you?" demanded Haledjian as a young man burst through the woods.

"Ed Magden. My house is about a hundred yards back there. I heard a shriek — what's happened?"

"Where were you an hour ago?" inquired Haledjian.

"Over at the boat yard. I'd just entered my driveway when I heard a shriek," replied Magden. "Here — what's this?"

Magden pointed to a metallic object partly buried under the coals. With a quick stride, he reached the pit, thrust in his hand, and pulled out a charred earring.

"Why, it's mine," gasped Nora. Suddenly her expression hardened. "Ed Magden, you hated Bill. What are you trying to do?"

"You hated him more than anyone," snapped back Magden.

"You hated enough to kill," Haledjian said to —

WHICH ONE?

Solution

Ed Magden, who claimed to have just arrived. Yet he knew the coals were sufficiently cool for him to "thrust in" his hand among them. Haledjian reasoned he had planted the earring to throw suspicion on Nora.

6

The Case of
the Bathing Beauty

"Bill Doyle killed Kitty Parker, all right," said Sheriff Monahan. "The only question is, was it premeditated, or did he kill in a moment of insanity?

"Whichever the jury decides will determine whether he lives or dies," the sheriff added as he and Dr. Haledjian took seats in the courtroom.

As the spectators crowded in, the sheriff gave Haledjian the details of the case.

"Kitty broke off with Doyle three weeks ago. He still carried a torch. But she dated freely.

"On the day of her death, she left work at two P.M. It was blazing hot, and she walked to the lake carrying her bathing suit wrapped in a towel. A lot of the young fellows noticed her. They had to — she was wearing a white blouse, tight gold toreador pants, and high-heeled gold sandals.

"There's an empty shack at the lake that's used as a place to change. Kitty got into her bikini and folded her clothes on the single bench.

"About three o'clock another girl reached the shack and discovered Doyle strangling Kitty. He insisted he was trying to revive her, and that he'd seen a tramp running away a moment before.

"At headquarters Doyle confessed to killing Kitty himself. 'She wouldn't come back to me,' he said. 'So I tried to scare her. I snatched her slip from among her clothes and wound it around her neck. She struggled . . . it was an accident!'

"Now," concluded the sheriff, "we'll see if the jury believes he only meant to scare her."

"They won't," said Haledjian.

WHY NOT?

Solution

Obviously, Doyle had brought along a slip to use in strangling Kitty, believing, if caught, he might blame her murder on blind impulse.

But Kitty would never have worn a slip that day. Not underneath a pair of tight toreador pants.

The Case of
the Big Dipper

"Curtis Brown was shot to death between ten and eleven o'clock last night," Inspector Winters told Dr. Haledjian.

"The body was found at midnight in the kitchen of his home by his mother. She telephoned headquarters at once.

"Brown was a wealthy bachelor. His estate will be divided evenly between his mother and Tim Brown, a nephew. That automatically makes Tim suspect number one."

"Has he an alibi?" inquired Haledjian.

"He claims he never left the roof of his house from nine last night till four this morning," replied the inspector. "Tim's recently become a camera fiend. He says he spent the night photographing the stars."

The inspector handed Haledjian a folder thick with large photographs of the heavens.

"Tim says he was taking these pictures at the time of the murder," the inspector went on. "His house is a two-hour drive from his uncle's."

The inspector tapped a photograph marked "one-hour exposure."

"He insists he took this picture between nine thirty and ten-thirty last night."

Haledjian studied the photograph — a beautifully clear shot of the Big Dipper.

The inspector said, "If Tim really clicked his

lens on at nine-thirty and off at ten-thirty, he couldn't have traveled two hours and killed his uncle between ten and eleven."

"I'm not an astrologist," replied Haledjian. "But from reading the stars in this photograph, I predict a cloudy future for Mr. Tim Brown!"

WHY?

Solution

Tim Brown could not have made a "beautifully clear shot" of the Big Dipper with his lens open an hour. The camera would have moved, due to the rotation of the earth, causing the stars on the photograph to appear as lines!

The Case of
the Birdwatcher

The body in the woods brought Dr. Haledjian's early morning nature walk to an abrupt end.

As he reached the summit of a little rise, he found Arthur Bently, well-known nature writer and a lifelong birdwatcher, lying on the downward slope. Death was due to a high-powered rifle bullet that had entered at the base of the skull.

Ascertaining that the killing had occurred about an hour before, or around seven A.M., Haledjian retraced Bently's steps. The rains of the previous night had washed the dirt trail smooth, and Bently's fresh footprints were easy to follow.

The trail led due west with arrowlike straightness back to Bently's summer bungalow.

Bob Hilton, the dead man's secretary, collapsed into a fireside chair when he heard the news.

"What was Bently doing out in the woods by himself?" questioned Haledjian.

"He went off birdwatching," said Hilton. "He liked to go out alone."

"Did you hear a shot?"

"Yes, but this is hunting season. The sound of guns is quite common," replied Hilton. "It must have been an accident. Mr. Bently had no enemies."

"I'll have to call the police," said Haledjian. "And while they're getting here, you'd better think up a better story than the one you told me!"

HOW COME?

Solution

Bently had been walking due east when he was shot. His direction gave the lie to Hilton's claim that he had gone off birdwatching.

An experienced birdwatcher like Bently would never walk due east, or into the rising sun, for he would perceive only the silhouettes of the birds against the bright sky!

The Case of
the Black Hat

Inspector Winters handed Dr. Haledjian a woman's crumpled black hat.

"In fashion lingo, it's called chic," said the inspector. "To me it's a clue — the only one — to the murderer of Marcia Davenport."

"The society beauty who was discovered early this morning near Route 22, strangled to death?" asked Haledjian.

"Yes. She was found wearing a sequinned black evening gown, satin pumps, a mink wrap, and black gloves — and she was bareheaded."

The inspector switched on his office intercom. "Bring in Ken Fowler."

Fowler, a handsome young man, glowered defiantly. Answering the inspector's question, he snapped, "Sure I left the party early last night — I hate those fancy shindigs. But I didn't take Marcia home in my car. I went alone."

"We have a witness," said the inspector. "Bill Betts, Marcia's escort. He insists she left early, with you. We found this hat in your car. I've already shown it to Betts, and he says he thinks it's the one she was wearing when she left. And her roommate says it was Marcia's hat, all right."

"Anybody could have stolen the hat and planted it in my car," growled Fowler.

"You were in love with Miss Davenport?"

"Yes — and so were half the men at the formal last night. Including your prize witness, Bill Betts."

Dismissing Fowler after a few more questions, the inspector asked Haledjian for his opinion.

"I think you can make an arrest," said the criminologist.

ARREST WHOM?

Solution

doesn't wear a hat with an evening gown.

Unfortunately for the jealous Betts, a woman Marcia Davenport having worn it to the formal. hat in his rival's car and concocted the story of Bill Betts. Haledjian knew he'd planted the

14

The Case of
the Bushwhackers

As the little burro tossed and jolted, Haledjian wondered what madness had prompted him to sign up for this mountain ride. He should have remained at the resort astride a beach chaise and let local color alone.

"That there's the Johnny Kid's corner," suddenly announced the tour's grizzly little guide. He pointed to a projection of rock which formed a perfect corner. "Seventy years ago on that spot, Ringo Charlie got bushwhacked by Johnny Kid.

"Johnny Kid objected to Ringo Charlie's weakness for palmin' aces. As Ringo Charlie was the fastest gun in three counties and related to half the town, Johnny Kid never pushed his objections. But one fine day he crouched behind that there rock and waited."

The guide dismounted and briefly made like Johnny Kid.

" 'Long about four in the afternoon," he resumed, "Ringo Charlie and his brother Sy come along. They'd suspicion'd somethin'. So they'd left the horses back a piece and come up quiet, on foot."

The guide rose from his knee, rounded the corner, and walked a dozen paces. He turned about, enacting the part of Ringo Charlie, and sneaked toward the corner. He squinted dramatically into the afternoon sun and held one hand cupped above the butt of an imaginary pistol.

"Johnny Kid seen Ringo Charlie's shadow comin' while Ringo was still six feet away. Out jumps the Kid, two guns blazin'. Ringo Charlie goes flat as a slab, and Sy hightails it back to town for a posse.

"A fair fight was one thing, but bushwhackin' was another breed of cow. When folks heerd how Johnny Kid had the advantage on Ringo Charlie, they up and lynched him, even though the Kid don't yet have any chin fuzz."

"They hanged an innocent boy," spoke up Haledjian.

The guide stared. "W-what's that?"

"Sy lied to the townsfolk. I suppose he hated to admit a mere boy beat his brother to the draw," said Haledjian.

WHAT WAS AMISS WITH THE STORY SY TOLD THE TOWNSFOLK?

Solution

Sy said Johnny Kid knew his brother was coming because at four o'clock his shadow, falling ahead of him, gave him away. Yet the guide, in retracing Ringo Charlie's approach, had "squinted . . . into the afternoon sun." With the sun in his face, Ringo Charlie's shadow would have fallen *behind him.*

16

The Case of
the Body by the Garage

The bulb hung directly above the up-turned hood of a white sports car. Through the open garage doors the dim yellow light reached into the night and illuminated the body of a man dressed in oil-splotched loafers, greasy wool shirt, and dirty blue jeans.

He might have been slumbering, except that his head was savagely crushed in.

"Roger Pratt, the socialite playboy," said Inspector Winters. "Mrs. Pratt's nurse saw the whole thing. It was she who summoned the police."

Inside the house, Bertha Tone, the nurse, repeated her story for Dr. Haledjian.

"I was with Mrs. Pratt all night. Mr. Pratt said she was not to be left alone. She's been very ill.

"About midnight I glanced through the bedroom window and saw Mr. Pratt step out of the garage. A woman slipped from behind those bushes and struck him with some instrument over the head."

"Didn't Mr. Pratt notice his assailant's approach?"

"It all happened too swiftly. As Mr. Pratt stooped to tie his shoelaces, the woman darted up behind him. I don't think he saw or heard her. I immediately called the police from the telephone in the bedroom."

"You didn't leave the house tonight?"

"No," replied the nurse, stiffening.

The nurse's statement was confirmed by Mrs. Pratt. "Bertha made a telephone call about midnight. Whispered so I couldn't hear! A little later she answered the doorbell. Otherwise she didn't leave me. What's the girl been up to?"

"She went downstairs to open the door for Inspector Winters and me," said Haledjian. "And she's been up to murder!"

WHAT WAS WRONG WITH THE NURSE'S STORY?

Solution

In asserting the dead man stooped over to tie his shoelaces, Berta Tone lied damningly. Roger Pratt was wearing loafers.

She had no reason to lie unless involved in the crime.

The Case of
the Bogus Hero

"Last night I had my lines down pat — yet something went wrong," moaned Cyril Makin, the would-be ladykiller. "Marjorie saw right through me."

He sighed. "Marjorie is Marjorie Appelson. She's the daughter of old General William 'Wild Bill' Appelson, and she's positively fiip over war heroes. I was a veterinary's aide in Korea and never heard a gun go off. So I had to invent a gutsy, front-line story to score with her."

"Perhaps if you tell me exactly what you told her, I might detect your mistake," suggested Haledjian.

The youth looked embarrassed, but he repeated his trumped-up tale for Haledjian.

"I was in an advanced post with some mortarmen when suddenly I heard rustling in the woods to our left. As it was a hot, windless day, I guessed what caused the rustling — the enemy.

"Presently they charged us. But I'd alerted our boys, and we countered with everything we had. They retreated, leaving a hundred dead.

"I'd just picked up a pair of field glasses from a dead captain when somebody shouted, 'More coming!'

"A column of infantry was approaching. We were all set to hit 'em with mortars when I cried, 'Hold your fire! They're Americans!'

"Later, I explained to the colonel that I'd spotted his regimental flag flying. He shook my hand and declared but for my quick thinking, his whole regiment would have been wiped out by our mortars!"

As Cyril finished, Haledjian chuckled. "I don't wonder Miss Appelson didn't believe you."

WHY NOT?

Solution

As it was a "hot, windless day," the regimental flag could not have been "flying." Obviously, Cyril could not have identified a regimental flag, or any other flag, hanging limp.

The Case of
the Bomb Thrower

Lying in the tree house, young Jimmy Metz looked across the street and saw the lights go off in the house belonging to Brett Hall, the outspoken candidate for the state senate.

Jimmy checked his watch. Ten past midnight.

Deciding that a tree house wasn't such a hot place to spend the night after all, Jimmy was about to start for bed. Then he noticed the convertible.

It was creeping slowly along the deserted street, its lights out. As it passed under the street lamp, Jimmy saw a man behind the wheel, another standing in the back.

"Aim for the bay window," said the driver. "And don't throw a fifty-eight-footer."

"Don't worry," said the standing man.

He drew back his arm and threw. Then the car shot away in a roar of acceleration.

A moment later the bomb exploded on Brett Hall's lawn.

Inspector Winters, investigating the case, questioned young Jimmy at great length. But the boy could provide no further information.

"Hall has received several threatening letters during the campaign," the inspector told Dr. Haledjian later. "The bomb apparently was intended to explode inside the house, but the bomber misjudged the distance. I doubt if we'll ever catch him."

"You've got one excellent lead," said Haledjian. "I should concentrate on the local baseball teams. Start your questioning with the catchers."

HOW COME?

Solution

Everyone knows it's sixty feet, six inches from the pitching rubber to home plate, but only catchers call those low pitches which bounce in front of the plate "fifty-eight-footers."

The Case of
the Civil War Saber

"From the length of your face I deduce it was slapped by some young lady whose good opinion you were endeavoring to win, but which you lost instead," said Dr. Haledjian.

"Quite right, as usual," muttered Cyril Makin, the capsizing Casanova. "This time I even went out and got a prop — a saber — to lend my story authenticity.

"You've heard of General R. Horatio Abercrombie? The old walrus fought for the Union during the Civil War. His great-great-granddaughter, Matilda, is secretary of the Civil War Round Table. She won't give you a tumble unless your great-great-grandfather fought in the great American conflict too.

"Unfortunately," went on Cyril, "both my great-great-grandparents were London chimney sweeps. They never fought anything but soot. So to impress Matilda, I invented an ancestor, Lieutenant George Makin, 79th New York Highlanders.

"I told Matilda that at the first battle of Bull Run, when the commanding officer was killed, Lieutenant Makin took over the regiment and saved it from annihilation. Again, at the second battle of Bull Run, the year following, he rallied the troops despite the loss of one hundred and five men.

23

"The month after First Bull Run, the men of his company presented George with a saber. Here I showed Matilda the saber I'd purchased at a costumer's shop and had inscribed:

"*To Lt. G. Makin, for gallantry at First Bull Run, July 21, 1861, from the men of his company, in appreciation.*

"I was feeling pretty cocky when I gave her the blade —"

"And then she promptly gave you the gate," said Haledjian. "I hardly blame her!"

WHAT WAS CYRIL'S MISTAKE?

Solution

As the second battle of Bull Run did not occur until "the year following" the first, the men of Lt. Makin's company could not have known "the month after First Bull" that there would be a second battle. They would have inscribed the blade ". . . at Bull Run," and not ". . . at First Bull Run."

The Case of
the Dead Man's Medals

The death of John Marks III of heart failure deprived the world of one of its leading philanthropists.

Marks, the only child of a former governor, and a bachelor, had devoted most of his life to the welfare of underprivileged children throughout the world.

Dr. Haledjian was among the many mourners who visited the Marks home on the hottest day of the year.

After viewing the body in the bedroom, the famed sleuth passed through the sweltering, crowded living room and into the library.

Here were displayed the awards given the deceased by many heads of state for his work with children. Some of the medals, inlaid with jewels, were worth thousands of dollars.

Haledjian had just nodded at the uniformed guard in the room when somebody shouted for a doctor.

Haledjian and the guard hurried into the living room, which had been thrown into a great commotion.

A young man wearing a dark gabardine suit was carrying a young lady in his arms toward the front door.

When the photographer from the local paper hurried up, the young man at first looked flustered. Then he snapped: "Please, no pictures. This is the deceased's niece, Vivian Farns. Show some respect. Let me get her outside."

Quickly Haledjian directed the guard to detain the pair.

Then he raced back into the library in time to prevent a thief from making off with the valuable collection of medals.

WHAT MADE HALEDJIAN SUSPICIOUS?

Solution

The girl's fainting spell was obviously a decoy to lure the guard from the library. She could not have been the niece of the deceased man, who had been a bachelor and an only child.

The Case of
the Dead Recluse

The body of Mrs. Frieda Deck, eighty-nine years old, was discovered in the kitchen of her three-room apartment where she had lived as a recluse for fifty years.

Police found one of the gas jets of her four-jet range on. Death was established as due to gas poisoning from the jet.

According to neighborhood gossip, the elderly woman had a fortune in cash hidden in the apartment.

"It looked at first like murder in the course of attempted robbery," Inspector Winters told Dr. Haledjian. "But Mrs. Beck's pocketbook, containing $219, was untouched on a love seat in the next room. An intruder would have spotted it right away.

"The janitor says a bill collector had asked him to investigate after finding the apartment door locked. The janitor says he refused, because Mrs. Beck had left strict orders never to be disturbed. He did nothing for an hour. Then, realizing he hadn't seen Mrs. Beck for longer than usual, he grew worried. Accompanied by the beat policeman, he unlocked the door. She was already dead."

"Was the apartment ransacked?" asked Haledjian.

"It was neat as a pin. But the window to the

fire escape in the living room was unlocked," replied the inspector. "Since the janitor is the only person with a key beside the victim, we're holding him on suspicion. He insists he's innocent."

"I'm sure he is," said Haledjian. "Death was accidental. Only a master murderer could have staged such a scene."

WHAT DID HALEDJIAN MEAN?

Solution

Only an experienced killer, after searching the apartment for the rumored fortune, would have tidied things up, ignored the cash in the pocketbook, and turned off three jets to make death look accidental.

The amateur killer would have turned on all four jets — and left them on — to make sure of the job.

The Case of
Death by the Tracks

The fat man lay by the railroad embankment, his horribly twisted limbs testifying to the imprudence of leaving a train as it raced at a hundred miles per hour.

"Broken neck — probably killed on impact," said Dr. Haledjian after a summary examination. "Who is he?"

"Tommy Warner, the New York racketeer," replied Sheriff Monahan. "He must have jumped from the Rocket. It leaves Chicago for Los Angeles on Tuesday night and passes through here around four Wednesday afternoon. It's the only train by today."

"What makes you sure Warner jumped?" asked Haledjian.

"For one thing, the money in his wallet. For another, his valises."

"Valises?"

"I'll show you," said the sheriff, shading his eyes as he led the way down the tracks toward the setting sun.

After some five hundred yards, the two men came to the first valise. It contained expensive clothes, monogrammed TW.

Two hundred yards farther along lay the second valise. It contained $50,000 in new twenty-dollar bills.

"Counterfeit," said the sheriff. "Apparently

someone wanted it, and Warner decided to jump rather than give it up."

"At least that's what someone wants the authorities to believe," said Haledjian. "The killer went to a lot of trouble, but Warner was thrown from the train."

HOW DID HALEDJIAN KNOW?

Solution

The two valises were found far to the west of the body ("toward the setting sun"), in the same direction as the train traveled (Chicago to Los Angeles).

Hence, Warner had left the speeding train first and his bags had followed him several seconds later.

The Case of
Death in the Air

The ancient tri-prop airplane had barely taken off from Nigeria when it encountered violent turbulence. After half an hour in the air, Dr. Haledjian's hopes of completing the bumpy trip in undisturbed misery were shattered by the steward.

"Come quickly, Dr. Haledjian!"

Musing on the inconveniences of fame, Haledjian groped along the storm-tossed cabin. In the front seat, a man sat lifeless, a knife in his heart.

Near the death seat was a small desk. On it lay a pad of legal-size sheets filled out in perfect handwriting.

"I was doing my manifests," said the steward. "Five minutes ago I heard a grunt, but thought nothing of it. A moment ago, I turned around and found passenger Alo like that."

Haledjian walked back up the aisle. The nine-seat plane held only three other passengers. All appeared to be dozing.

In the middle of the plane a fat man sat in stocking feet. One shoe lay on the seat beside him, the other on the floor.

The last two seats were occupied by a young couple. The man held the girl by the left wrist. She sat rigidly, teeth bared, as if suffering from fright.

31

Haledjian advised the pilot to alert the police, and when the plane landed, he told the officer in charge: "Arrest —"

WHOM?

Solution

The steward. He could not have filled out the manifest with "perfect handwriting" during the storm-tossed flight.

The Case of
the Doubting Uncle

"Are you sure no one has entered this room since your uncle's suicide?" asked Dr. Haledjian.

"Positive," replied young Lloyd Carstairs. "I have the only key."

It had been four days since Henry Fitzsimmons had taken his own life. He had left notes for the two men who now prepared to enter his bedroom.

In the notes, Fitzsimmons requested that a four-day waiting period be observed before the room was entered and the safe behind his portrait opened.

The $100,000 therein was to be divided equally between his alma mater and his only kin, young Carstairs.

Haledjian walked to the fireplace above which hung the portrait of the deceased. A plant was set on the mantel, its broad leaves turned to the wall and touching the canvas.

Haledjian carefully removed the plant, lest he knock it over, and swung back the portrait.

"Suppose you open the safe," he said to Carstairs. "I believe your note included the combination too."

While the youth worked the dial, Haledjian crossed to the sunny window directly opposite the portrait. The window was locked from the inside.

There was a click. The youth cried, "The safe's empty!"

"Of course," said Haledjian. "I have the money, which your uncle sent me. He wanted to test you — to see if you'd try to open the safe before the four days elapsed."

"I never was in here!" insisted the youth.

"A bad lie," said Haledjian. "And a costly one. Now all the money will go to your uncle's alma mater."

WHAT WAS THE YOUTH'S MISTAKE?

Solution

The window was locked from the inside, and the youth had the only key. Hence it had to be he who, in secretly opening the safe, replaced the plant so that the leaves were "turned to the wall."

Untouched in four days, the leaves should have been turned toward the window and the sun.

The Case of
the Dowager's Jewels

Mrs. Sydney, the dowager who was reputed to own eight and a quarter percent of New York City, had gratified every whim but one.

She had never confounded the master sleuth, Dr. Haledjian.

So Haledjian was on his guard when, after a sip of Vichy water, Mrs. Sydney leaned back in her dinner chair and related her most recent harrowing experience.

"You shall hardly believe how close I came to losing my life and jewels last night," she began.

"It must have been around three A.M. when a noise awoke me. A masked man was standing in my room, pointing a gun at me and ordering me not to cry out.

"By the moonlight, I could see two more men climbing through the open window. I was bound and gagged and brutally thrown on my back on the bed while the horrible creatures went through my jewels.

"Helpless, I watched the fiends fill a sack with gems. For fear of my life, I did not dare do anything till they had started out the window.

"As the last of them went out, I screamed for help. Fortunately, Patrolman Casey was a block away and heard me. The thieves dropped the jewels in their haste to escape from him, but I shall be a month recovering from the fright!"

Haledjian smiled appreciatively.

"My dear Mrs. Sydney," he said. "Your convalescence from an experience that never happened will undoubtedly be short."

WHAT WAS WRONG WITH HER STORY?

Solution

As Mrs. Sydney was "helpless," having been bound and "gagged," it would have been impossible for her to cry out loud enough for Patrolman Casey, "a block away," to have heard her.

The Case of
the Dropped Cuff Link

"My latest case," said Sheriff Monahan to Dr. Haledjian "required some rapid deduction that would have done you credit."

The sheriff leaned back in his chair, took a long drag on his cigar, and with an air of contentment recounted the details.

"A single gunman held up Brigs and Company and escaped with the entire monthly payroll. I got a tip that he would be aboard a train headed for Columbia, South Carolina, that afternoon.

"I caught the train. Unfortunately, I didn't know what my man looked like. I could only keep watch for anyone acting suspiciously.

"The conductors helped me. They reported that the occupant of lower nine in car eleven fifty-five was the only passenger who kept his face hidden. He had poked his ticket through the curtain of his berth.

"To get a look at him, I took the berth above his, and purposefully dropped a cuff link down on him. There was no place for him to hide — not with me suddenly hanging head down next to him.

"Alas, he was reading a newspaper, held full length before him. I told him about the cuff link, and he told me to 'beat it,' without showing his face.

"I thought I'd flubbed till I caught a glance at the headlines of his paper: LONE BANDIT ESCAPES WITH 100G PAYROLL."

"You arrested him, I presume?" asked Haledjian.

"On the spot," replied the sheriff.

WHAT GAVE THE HOLDUP
MAN AWAY?

Solution

The fact that the sheriff, hanging head down, could read the headlines at a glance meant that the newspaper was turned the same way. Hence the man in lower nine was "reading" it upside down!

The Case of

Edmund Bayne

Dr. Haledjian was driving past the small home of Edmund Bayne, a retired army officer, when he saw a young man dash out the front door.

"Help!" he shouted. "Somebody get a doctor!"

Haledjian offered his services, and the youth hurried him into the house.

Beside the telephone table in the foyer lay the body of Edmund Bayne.

"Who is he?" exclaimed the young man. "Are you a friend?"

"Yes — he was Ed Bayne. Don't you know him?"

The youth shook his head. "Never heard of him."

"Ed's been retired for fifteen years," said Haledjian. "I didn't think he had an enemy in the world. How did you happen to find him?"

"I was running for the bus when I heard a shot from this house. I found the front door unlocked and him lying like that."

Haledjian's swift examination disclosed that death, from a bullet wound in the heart, had occurred within the past few minutes. A French Army pistol lay beside the body.

"Call the police," advised Haledjian. "The number is 666-4551."

The youth dialed and spoke excitedly.

"Hello, police? Somebody shot Edmund Bayne! Where? Oh, on High Street . . . middle of the block . . . brick house . . . ah . . ."

"The address is 621 High Street," said Haledjian. "As if you don't know!"

WHY DID HE DOUBT THE YOUTH?

Solution

The youth claimed he had "never heard" of Edmund Bayne. Yet he told the police the dead man's first name was Edmund.

As Haledjian had told him only "Ed," he could not have known whether it was Edmund, Edward, Edwin, or Edgar!

The Case of
the Fatal Oversight

It took only five minutes on a hot August night for Johnson to kill Kuto and rob him of $3,000.

Six minutes before eleven P.M., the time the main feature at the corner movie theater began, Johnson stepped across the hall and knocked at Kuto's door.

Being admitted, Johnson closed the door behind him. Kuto stared questioningly at Johnson's black-gloved hands; his eyes opened wide as Johnson drew his gun. The silencer whistled twice. Kuto fell.

Taking the dead man's keys, Johnson opened Kuto's strongbox and put $3,000 in cash into his pocket. Then he dialed the police.

"My name is Johnson," he said. "I'm calling from Mr. Kuto's apartment at 591 Grand Street. There's been a murder!"

Hanging up, Johnson slipped out of Kuto's apartment, dropped the gun down the garbage chute, and went across the hall to his own room. There he removed his gloves and hid the money.

He was waiting in Kuto's room when Inspector Winters arrived. He said: "It was too hot to sleep, so I decided to go to a movie. As I stepped into the hall, a big man dashed out of Kuto's door, knocked me down, tossed some-

41

thing into the garbage chute, and raced downstairs."

That night the inspector related the case to Dr. Haledjian, concluding with: "Johnson claimed he had not been in Kuto's apartment for a week. But after our lab boys got through there, Johnson confessed. I suppose you can guess why."

HALEDJIAN GUESSED. CAN YOU?

Solution

Although Johnson telephoned from Kuto's apartment, his fingerprints were not on the telephone.

He did not remove his gloves till after entering his own apartment — a fatal oversight on a hot August night!

The Case of
the Five Candidates

"Charles was going to announce his successor as president of Consolidated Coal and Oil at our home tonight," Mrs. Charles Twayne, widow of the murdered man, told Haledjian.

"Each of the five young men invited to dinner was a candidate," she continued. "However, as Charles left for the golf club this morning, he said he might eliminate one."

"At lunch time," interrupted Sheriff Monahan, "Mr. Twayne and Rick Donovan had an argument in the men's grille. Was Donovan the one eliminated, Mrs. Twayne?"

"I don't know," she replied. "Charles didn't say which one. When he came to the tenth tee, he saw me standing on the terrace and held up four fingers. 'Four!' he called to me, meaning I should set the table for four guests instead of five. A moment later he clutched his chest and toppled over."

"The killer used a silencer," said the sheriff. "I took a statement from Rick Donovan two hours after the shooting. He claims he left the club without knowing of Mr. Twayne's death."

Haledjian picked up Donovan's statement, written in the suspect's own hand. He glanced through it till he came to:

"I was playing the eighteenth and had hooked my drive into the bushes behind the

43

tenth tee. As I searched for the ball, I heard Twayne shout, 'Four!' But I didn't see him because of the bushes. And, as I returned to my home without changing clothes, I knew nothing of his death for two hours."

"Donovan is lying," declared Haledjian. "Undoubtedly he was the one eliminated by Mr. Twayne for the presidency and took revenge by murder."

WHAT TRIPPED DONOVAN?

Solution

Donovan asserted he did not see Twayne on the tee, yet he knew Twayne shouted, "Four!" Obviously, he'd seen Twayne signal his wife, or he would have written that Twayne shouted the golfer's warning, "Fore!"

The Case of
the Football Player

Dr. Haledjian and Sheriff Monahan sloshed ankle-deep in the chill waters of huge Lake Tomanachi as they walked by the outside of the nine-foot wall set in the sandy shallows behind the murdered woman's house.

"The wall completely encloses the house," said the sheriff. "Two hours ago, John Bookman came home from a late movie. He thought he saw a man going over the wall here."

The sheriff pointed to a homemade ladder leaning against the outside of the wall.

"It was pitch dark, and so Bookman decided he was imagining things — you'll notice the top of the ladder is four inches below the top of the wall, and so it can't be seen from the house side. Then he discovered his wife in the kitchen, stabbed to death.

"Bookman suspects her ex-boyfriend, Gary Mills, a professional football tackle, who has a cottage across the lake. Mills, who owns a rowboat, insists he was home all night, but he has no corroborating witness."

Haledjian climbed the ladder, looked at the back of the Bookman house, and climbed down. The top of the ladder was now six inches below the top of the wall.

"Shall I arrest Mills?" asked the sheriff.

"No, Bookman," snorted Haledjian.

Solution

The ladder was an obvious prop to mislead the police.

No one — certainly not a ponderous professional tackle like Gary Mills — could have used it, since Haledjian's weight on it, after it supposedly had been used, caused the ladder to sink two inches more — from "four inches below the top of the wall" to "six inches."

The Case of
the Four-Footed Sleuth

"I suppose the Brandywine case is the only murder ever solved with the help of a chipmunk," said Dr. Haledjian.

"Sounds fascinating. Tell me about it!" begged Octavia.

"A highway patrolman," began the criminologist, "was driving in a sudden thunderstorm on Lakeview Drive when he spied an old, green convertible, top down, parked on a dirt side road.

"The fact that the convertible was empty, yet the horn was honking in wild spurts, caused the officer to investigate.

"The mystery seemed closed when he discovered a chipmunk had caught its hind leg in the horn mechanism. The officer freed the poor creature and as a matter of course noted down the car's license number.

"Two weeks later the body of Sylvia Brandywine was found on the other side of the hill from the spot at which the convertible had been parked. Death, due to strangulation, had occurred about the day the convertible was sighted.

"The police backchecked and questioned the car's owner, Oscar Hayes, a pipe fitter. He admitted being out by the lake. However, he said he'd left the convertible when he couldn't start it. He denied leaving the car to hide the body.

"Phil Burger, manager of Ace Garage, said Hayes telephoned him to get the car. Burger found the battery absolutely dead and towed the car back to town.

"Burger and the police agreed Hayes was making his call about the time the convertible was found by the patrolman.

"Now," concluded Haledjian. "I was quite sure Hayes was lying — that he probably was off hiding the body of Miss Brandywine when the patrolman sped the car."

WHAT WAS THE GIVEAWAY?

Solution

accomplice.
not have made the horn honk. Burger was an
been "absolutely dead" or the chipmunk could
couldn't start it since the battery could not have
the top down in the rain. He lied in saying he
Hayes needed an alibi for leaving his car with

48

The Case of
the Frightened Playboy

Answering an urgent telephone summons from the playboy, Jeff Lawry, Dr. Haledjian arrived at Lawry's penthouse a minute before seven A.M.

A tall woman was waiting at the penthouse door.

In a moment Haledjian and the tall woman were admitted by Lawry, who was clad in a bathrobe and green pajamas. He greeted Dr. Haledjian and stared suspiciously at the woman.

"I'm Clara Miley," she said. "The agency sent me."

"The new maid," exclaimed Lawry, obviously relieved. "Your room is that one. The kitchen is in the rear. I was about to have something to eat. Do you mind fixing me something?"

The woman strode off obediently. Lawry led Haledjian into the study and carefully closed the door.

"I've lived in absolute terror," confided the playboy, "since I saw those men rob the bank last week. Do you know what I've been doing? Sleeping days and sneaking out nights!"

"Suppose we talk with Inspector Winters at headquarters," suggested Haledjian. "He'll give you protection."

"Not this morning," said Lawry wearily. "I've been awake all night. I'm going to bed."

Just then Clara Miley entered the study with a tray.

"I've fixed you a snack, sir," she said.

"That looks just fine," said Lawry, glancing at the glass of milk, ham sandwich, and layer cake. He picked up the milk.

"Don't drink it!" shouted Haledjian, seizing the new maid.

WHAT ALARMED HALEDJIAN?

Solution

Only someone aware of Lawry's recent night habits would have prepared a "snack" of milk, sandwich, and cake at seven A.M.

Had Clara Miley really been just a maid, she would have fixed him breakfast; i.e., coffee, juice, eggs, etc.

The Case of
the Frozen Suspect

When the bitter cold that had frozen most of the Tahoo River practically all winter began to pass, a small boy noticed something red just below the surface.

It turned out to be a scarf — wrapped around the neck of a man. The body was further clothed in thick-soled shoes, two sweaters, rough trousers, work gloves, and a brown stocking cap.

Bud Kobs, missing since the previous November, had come to shore encased in a tomb of ice.

Kobs had been wanted in the slaying of Otis Ware. Art Byrnes, a partner with Ware and Kobs in a junkyard by the river, had witnessesed the killing.

On the morning of November 23, while the men were moving a pile of pipes, Kobs and Ware fell to arguing, Byrnes had told the coroner's jury.

In a fit of rage, Byrnes said, Kobs had seized a three-foot length of cast iron pipe and hit Ware on the head. Tossing the pipe away, Kobs had dashed for the frozen river.

He got half way across, Byrnes said, and fell through the ice.

"Kobs couldn't swim," Sheriff Monahan told Dr. Haledjian the day after the body was found. "He must have banged his head on the ice and never regained consciousness. The autopsy showed a severe contusion on the base of the skull.

"Kobs had a criminal record," concluded the sheriff. "We matched his fingerprints against those on the pipe last November. He's the murderer, all right. Case closed!"

"Case nearly closed," corrected Haledjian.

WHY NOT CLOSED?

Solution

Haledjian deduced that Byrnes had slain both partners after contriving to get Kobs's fingerprints on the pipe.

His story of an argument was patently false, since when Kobs was found he was wearing "work gloves," and hence could not have left fingerprints on the pipe during a fight.

The Case of
the Gas Station Murder

All the money — $14.19 — that Cal Peak had in his pockets when he was gunned down was spread on Sheriff Monahan's desk.

Dr. Haledjian fingered a two-dollar bill, one of four such. The rest of the money consisted of a five-dollar bill, a half-dollar, a quarter, four dimes, and four pennies.

"Odd that Peak should be carrying four two-dollar bills," said the famous sleuth. "Was there a reason?"

"No," replied the sheriff. "At least none that I can find. And there doesn't seem to be a reason for his killing.

"There was one witness," continued the sheriff. "Archie Kemp. Peak was sitting in Archie's gas station yesterday when, around noon, a man entered and asked for change. Archie didn't catch the sum, because just then he yawned. But Peak took out his money and said he could make change.

"Now here's the queer part," said the sheriff. "Archie heard the stranger say that he'd left his money in his car. So Peak followed him outside. Archie saw the stranger walk to a big yellow convertible. There was another man behind the wheel; he pulled a gun and shot Peak twice in cold blood. Then the convertible roared off.

Archie was so dumbfounded he didn't even get the license number."

"For a good reason," said Haledjian. "Archie's account is a complete lie."

HOW DID HALEDJIAN KNOW?

Solution

Archie said that Peak "took out his money and said he could make change" for the stranger. Impossible. He couldn't have made change for any bill or coin with the $14.19 found on his corpse.

The Case of
the Gasping Partner

Dr. Haledjian glanced at his watch — ten minutes to midnight — as he answered the telephone.

"Hello? This is Ben Bird!" came the excited voice. "I was just speaking to Clyde Linz on the telephone when I heard him gasp — then nothing. Something's happened! Can you meet me at his apartment right away?"

"I can be there in fifteen minutes," said the sleuth.

Bird and Linz, partners in a roofing business, lived in the fine old section of the city. Bird was waiting on the sidewalk when Haledjian arrived in a taxi.

They rode the elevator to Linz's floor. "I've got a key," said Bird, unlocking the door to Linz's small bachelor abode.

Linz was dead on the couch. A knife protruded from his chest.

Death had occurred within the hour, Haledjian found.

"Clyde telephoned me as I was going to bed," said Bird. "He said something urgent had come up. He wanted to speak with me right away. Suddenly he gave a hideous gasp. I dialed you immediately."

Haledjian noted the open window leading to the fire escape.

The telephone receiver hung off the cradle near the dead man's right hand.

"I'll notify the police," said Haledjian. "But before I do, you'd better stop lying!"

WHY DID HE DOUBT BIRD?
(Look out. A toughie.)

Solution

Linz and Bird lived in the "fine old section of the city." Bird claimed that Linz telephoned him.

But Bird also claimed that he telephoned Haledjian "immediately" afterward. Impossible! In the old sections of the city (pre-1957) only the person originating a telephone call can terminate it.

Linz's telephone was still off the hook. Therefore, Bird must have been holding a dead line!

The Case of
the Gold Brick

"My great-grandfather, Everet Lamont Sydney, panned gold from a secret stream and by 1875 was the richest man in California," said Mrs. Sydney, a sly twinkle in her eye.

"On his death bed, he told two old prospectors, Jepp Hanson and Oscar Tyre, the way to the stream and agreed to let them pan for gold, provided they swore never to divulge the location or make more than one trip themselves.

"Jepp and Oscar signed a contract, which stated: 'Whatever gold Jepp Hanson and Oscar Tyre or any individual in their expedition can carry by himself from the stream to the home of Everet Sydney shall be given said individual.'

"Naturally, Jepp and Oscar didn't bring anyone else in on their bonanza. They set out by themselves the next morning, having loaded Jepp's old mule with enough tools and provisions to stay in the wilds six months.

"They had hardly got to the stream when a landslide buried their equipment. All the two prospectors salvaged were the shorts they wore at night, the mule, and two pans.

"Since the contract said they could make only one trip, they stayed on, living off wild berries and nuts. After five months they got enough gold dust, which, to prevent being blown, they ingeniously melted into a brick. That small brick, measuring but a foot long, six inches wide, and six inches high, would make them millionaires.

"My great-grandfather died while they were away, and the two oldtimers took their case to court. Each insisted he had been the one who carried the brick.

"The judge peered at the brick and at the contract, and awarded the gold — to whom?"

Dr. Haledjian shook his head reproachfully. "My dear Mrs. Sydney. You are forever trying to trip up an old sleuth."

And so that the other guests couldn't hear, he whispered, "To —"

TO WHOM?

Solution

The mule. Neither oldtimer could have carried the brick more than ten yards. A brick of gold, measuring one foot long by six inches wide by six inches high weighs over three hundred pounds.

The Case of
the Happy Baby

"John Wilson doesn't look much like a murderer," said Sheriff Monahan as a young man emerged from the farmhouse carrying a naked baby boy.

The sheriff stopped the patrol car behind Wilson's yellow sedan. He drew his pistol, whispered to Dr. Haledjian to wait, and called: "Raise your hands, John!"

Wilson halted, amazed. He sat his infant son carefully on the fender of his car and lifted his hands. "What's it all about, Sheriff?"

"Murder. We have a witness who says you entered Moose Long's bar last night after closing. Half an hour later Mrs. Long found Moose strangled to death with a yellow scarf."

"That's a lie. Why —"

"Look out!" cried Haledjian, as the baby scampered onto the yellow hood. Cooing happily, he attempted to stand. Haledjian just saved him from toppling to the ground.

"That witness is mistaken, Sheriff," Wilson resumed calmly. "I've been in this car since eight o'clock last night driving down from Philadelphia. I just arrived five minutes ago."

The sheriff looked at his watch. "Then you drove the six hundred miles between Philly and here in a little over twelve hours," he said dubiously.

"Can you prove I didn't?" snapped Wilson.

"Nothing could be easier," declared Haledjian.

WHAT WAS WRONG WITH WILSON'S ALIBI?

Solution

If Wilson had really arrived home "five minutes ago," having driven six hundred miles, the motor — and the hood — of his car would still be sizzling hot. The baby would have been screaming, not "cooing happily" standing on the hood.

The Case of
Hidden Money

"Doc Everette is down with the flu," said Sheriff Kimball. "I hated to call you on such a hot day, but I need someone to sign the death certificate."

"Any reason to support foul play?" inquired Dr. Haledjian, kneeling beside the body of the wizened old recluse.

"None whatever. Old Carl lived up here alone with his cats. Sort of a character, you know, but harmless. He used to drive to town in a flivver once a week. Since he got the deep freeze installed last year, he came in every other month."

"When was his last trip?"

"Oh, maybe seven — eight weeks ago."

"I suppose the old man disliked banks as well as people?"

"There was that story. Life savings hidden under the floorboards somewhere. The usual stuff. Some folks in town believed it."

"Judging by the body temperature, he's been dead about twelve hours," said Haledjian. "In lay terms, he died of plain old age. Incidentally, who found the body?"

"Jim Casey, when he delivered the mail half an hour ago."

Haledjian stepped to the table where the sheriff had laid out the articles found in the dead man's pockets. There were two small fish for the cats, an antique pocket watch, and a dollar and ten cents in coins.

Haledjian picked up the fish, sniffed, and swiftly passed them a foot under the sheriff's nose. "Smell anything extraordinary?"

"No — just a faint fishy odor."

"That's what is extraordinary," replied Haledjian. "I'll have to request an autopsy, Sheriff. Old Carl's death is not what it appears!"

WHAT WAS THE BASIS FOR HALEDJIAN'S REQUEST?

Solution

After being twelve hours in Old Carl's pocket on a hot day, the fish would have smelled to high heaven.

Haledjian suspected that the nearly empty deep freeze (last trip to town seven weeks ago) had been used to lower the old man's body temperature quickly. Thus death was made to appear as occurring hours earlier.

The Case of
the Impoverished Artist

The body of Monroe Sheld, an impover-
ished sixty-year-old painter, lay over a table in
his sweltering one-room apartment. A bullet had
entered his right temple. On his right side, by
the leg of his chair, was an old-fashioned, single
action revolver.

The table was bare except for a cracked
plate, a saucerless cup, knife, fork, and spoon,
and an overturned salt shaker.

"Sheld has been peddling his sketches for a
dollar or two in the local bars," said Inspector
Winters. "His doctor says he was stricken with
heart failure two months ago and nearly died.
You might say he ate a last meal and committed
suicide."

"Correction," said Dr. Haledjian. "There was
a bit about him in today's paper. A small but
fashionable art gallery announced a one-man
showing of his paintings next month. He had
everything to live for."

Haledjian opened a small cupboard layered
with dust. One plate and cup, and a setting of
cheap silverware, however, were quite clean.
Next he opened a paper garbage bag and sniffed.

"This food was put in the bag within the past
three hours, or about the time of Sheld's death,"
asserted Haledjian. "Longer than that and it

would have begun to spoil and smell in this heat."

Haledjian shut the bag. "I shouldn't close the case quite yet, Inspector. Sheld had a dinner guest who tried to cover up his presence here."

WHAT MADE HALEDJIAN SO CERTAIN?

Solution

Sheld, having suffered a heart failure, would have watched his diet carefully. He never would have brought salt to the table unless it was for another's use.

The Case of
the Initialed Tie Clasp

Leo Murtag had been floating in the East River for three days when his corpse was fished out by the police.

"Whoever killed him nearly botched the job," Inspector Winters told a battery of reporters. "The killer first attempted to strangle him with Murtag's own bow tie. Apparently when that didn't work, he resorted to a forty-inch piece of tarred hemp rope — the kind used for marine purposes. It did the job properly.

"Murtag's pockets were empty," the inspector continued. "When found, he had on a white shirt with French cuffs and blue trousers, but no jacket."

An hour after the first editions hit the streets, Nick the Nose was banging on the inspector's door. He had, as usual, information to peddle.

"I found this," the grimy little informer said. He held out a tie clasp fashioned in the shape of a catboat. On the back was engraved, "To LM from GB."

"LM is Leo Murtag and GB is Gina Bettina, his old flame," volunteered Nick.

"Could be Gina," conceded the inspector. "We'll never know. She commited suicide last month. Where'd you find the clasp?"

"That bit of information will cost you," snapped Nick. "I figure if you knew where he lost the clasp, you'd know where he was attacked, and if —"

"Enough!" roared the inspector. "I'll pay — with this!"

He drove the toe of his shoe into the seat of Nick's pants.

"He deserves worse," commented Haledjian, opening the door as Nick flew by.

WHY WAS NICK GIVEN THE BOOT?

Solution

Nick's tie clasp was obviously a fake clue. Murtag would not have used one, for he was wearing a bow tie when slain.

The Case of
the Italian Grocer

The death of Joseph Pastrono, a grocer, might have passed for suicide but for the keen eye of Dr. Haledjian.

Pastrono had come to America from Italy as a boy of nine years. His family being poor, he had left school in the fourth grade to go to work.

He had married and raised two sons. Although of limited education, he faithfully read the news every evening in an Italian language newspaper.

His body was found above his grocery store, in the tidy four-room apartment where he had lived alone since the death of his wife Anna the year before. He had apparently shot himself with the revolver he usually kept in his store for protection.

The police found no substance to the rumors that he had hidden his life savings somewhere in his apartment.

Beside Pastrono's body was a suicide note, written, his sons were convinced, in his handwriting. It read:

"I am tired and sick. My body pains me every hour of the day. The doctors say nothing can be done; I am too old. If I were twenty years younger, I'd try to go on. But my Anna is dead, and my sons have families of their own. I do not wish to be a nuisance. This is the only solution for me. God forgive me!"

Haledjian put down the note and said, "Pastrono was murdered!"

HOW DID HE KNOW?

Solution

Haledjian perceived at once that the note was a forgery.

Pastrono, who had left school in the fourth grade and read an Italian newspaper instead of one in English, could not have written a note perfect in grammar (including the subjunctive mode), punctuation, and spelling!

The Case of
the Italian Sports Car

"Two days ago somebody with a dime-store mask tried to stick up the City Bank," said Sheriff Monahan.

"The hold-up man panicked and fled empty-handed," he added. "It must have been the heat that made him try it."

Dr. Haledjian glanced out the open window of the patrol car. "The weather seems normal for October."

"Today is like the rest of the twelve days of the month — sixty degrees," said the sheriff. "But yesterday and the day before — whew! It was a hundred degrees, and folks went batty."

The sheriff drew up in front of a pretentious home.

"The Vandergriffs's mansion," he explained. "Their son Ted is a suspect in the holdup attempt. A woman near the bank saw him driving his Italian sports car away at a breakneck speed. I thought you'd be interested in his story."

Ted, a long-haired teenager, insisted the witness had been seeing heat waves near the bank, not him.

"Nobody's driven this job in a week," he said. "I've been using the family Rolls."

"An Italian sports car with American luxury," commented Haledjian, noting the sports car's radio, air-conditioner, heater, and power windows.

"Power brakes and power steering too," said Ted. "Why not? It cost my father a cool ten grand."

Haledjian slid behind the wheel and started the engine.

Ted's face went white as a sudden noise from inside the car swept away his alibi.

CAN YOU GUESS THE NOISE?

Solution

A blast of air — from the air-conditioner. Ted had forgotten to turn it off. Despite his denial, he had obviously used the car during the two-day heat wave when the attempted bank holdup had occurred!

The Case of
the Kidnapped Brother

Jerry Hickman gazed dully across the room as Inspector Winters and Dr. Haledjian sought to question him.

"I know it's difficult," said the inspector patiently. "But try to remember everything you can. You may give us a clue to your kidnappers."

Hickman shook his head regretfully. "What I remember isn't much. Three men jumped me Wednesday night in front of my apartment. They shoved me into a car and chloroformed me.

"The next thing I knew I was lying on a stone floor. I lit a match and saw I was in a windowless room empty except for a chair and a cracked sink. The door was locked.

"I could hear the kidnappers talking. I learned they had asked my stepsister Harriet for fifty thousand dollars. I guess they'd read that she'd just inherited our father's estate, valued at half a million dollars.

"After a few hours, they left to collect the ransom. I tried yelling, but it was no use. I couldn't batter down the door. I thought to lift it off its hinges, but it hinged on the other side. There was nothing to do but wait.

"When the men returned, I could tell they'd been successful in collecting the ransom. And I felt sure they now intended to kill me. The ones called Frank and Monty went for the car. The one called Beno came for me.

"I hid behind the door as Beno pushed it cautiously into the room. He had a flashlight and gun, and I almost got to him with the upraised chair when he dodged. He must have cracked me with the gun. I don't remember anything till I regained consciousness outside Harriet's home three hours ago."

"A good thing the ransom bills were marked," Haledjian told the inspector after the interview. "As soon as Hickman spends some of them, you can arrest him for fraud."

WHY DID HALEDJIAN BELIEVE THE KIDNAPPING WAS STAGED?

Solution

Hickman said the door "hinged on the other side," and yet Beno "pushed it cautiously into the room." — a contradiction.

Beno would have pulled the door to himself, not pushed it into the room, since doors swing toward their hinged side.

The Case of
the Killer Dog

"It's so cold in here, there's no telling how long the old man's been dead," said Haledjian, turning to look out the window upon the snow covered slopes.

Three sets of footprints led to the cabin's door. From the south came the double tracks newly made by himself and Sheriff Monahan.

From the north were the tracks of a single visitor. They led up to the door and away from it.

All about were the paw prints of a huge dog.

"Those tracks to the north are Buff Carter's, I take it," said Haledjian.

"Correct," said the sheriff. "Buff brought old Jed's supplies about once a week. He said his last trip here was six days ago, right after the big snow. He got inside the door, he says, when Jed's mongrel attacked him. Buff swears he won't be back till Jed gets rid of the beast."

"Buff won't have any reason to come back," muttered Haledjian, looking down at the half naked body of Jed Tompkins.

"He must have been changing his clothes when his dog went loco and did that to his throat," mused the sheriff.

"Didn't Jed ever go outside?" asked Haledjian.

"Not since last September — that's when he

73

broke his legs," answered the sheriff.

Suddenly Haledjian saw a great, ugly dog following Buff Carter's tracks toward the cabin. The animal moved with its nose to the snow for several hundred feet.

"That dog is big enough," said Haledjian. "But I doubt if a dog did the killing."

WHAT AROUSED HALEDJIAN'S SUSPICION?

Solution

Buff Carter had claimed his "last trip . . . was six days ago," and yet his tracks were fresh enough to hold human odor. Had they been six days old, the dog would not have been sniffing them.

Haledjian believed Buff had staged the killing to make it appear as if the dog were the culprit.

The Case of
the Lakeside Murder

     "I need your opinion on the Topping murder," Sheriff Monahan said to Dr. Haledjian.

     "Topping was the guest of Arthur Blair," began the sheriff. "The Blair cottage is about a quarter mile from mine on Lake Gentsch. Two nights ago, as I was retiring, I heard a shot from there.

     "Hurrying outside, I met Blair running toward me. 'Come quickly!' he cried. 'Fritz Topping's been shot!'

     "As we started for his place, Blair told me, 'Fritz and I were watching the late news on television when all of a sudden the lights went out. I started up to investigate when the front door swung open. A man with a rifle shot Fritz and disappeared before I could recover my wits.

     "I saw Fritz had been shot in the heart and I ran directly to fetch you," concluded Blair.

     "The Blair cottage," the sheriff went on, "was dark. A little moonlight played in the living room where Fritz Topping sat in the chair. I had brought a flashlight and it took but an insant to confirm that he was dead.

     "Somebody had pulled the master fuse in the garage. When we replaced it, the kitchen light and a table lamp behind the corpse went on. I could see the body was slightly tilted away from the front door.

"I told Blair to try to recall what he could."

The cottage was silent for a full minute before Blair shook his head. "I-it happened so fast. I've told you everything I can remember."

"Which," broke in Haledjian, "should be enough to bring him to trial for murder!"

WHY?

Solution

Blair claimed that he and Topping had been watching television when the lights went out and the murder occurred. Yet when the master fuse was replaced, there was a "full minute" of silence in the cottage.

Had Blair been telling the truth, the television would have come back on with the lights.

The Case of
the Lobster Joint

In the kitchen of his restaurant, The Lobster Joint, the body of Al Peltz lay covered by a police blanket.

"Al was too generous," sobbed Mrs. Peltz, wife of the murdered man. "He fed every hobo who came to the door."

"We think robbery was the motive," said Sheriff Monahan gently. "Your husband's pockets were empty. Did he normally carry a lot of cash?"

"About two hundred dollars," replied Mrs. Peltz. "I think that fellow in the khaki shirt must have done this terrible thing. Five minutes before I discovered Al's body, I came into the kitchen to pick up an order for table six. Al was talking to this man — why, that's him!"

An unshaven little man wearing a dirty khaki shirt suddenly broke away from the crowd of curious onlookers outside the kitchen door. The sheriff shouted to a deputy who collared the fugitive and hauled him before Mrs. Peltz.

"Look, lady, I was here," the man gasped in fright. "But I didn't do nothin'. The fella with the apron said he'd give me something to eat. He put a big red lobster into the pan and told me to come back in twenty minutes."

"C'mon!" snapped the sheriff. "You realized that Mrs. Peltz had seen you, and that we'd

comb the county for you. A nice bluff coming
back here. Now where did you hide the
money?"

"I don't know nothin' about any money!"
wailed the man. "I wouldn't lie."

"What innocent person needs to," said Haledjian with a sigh. "And yet a whopper has been
told in this room!"

WHO LIED?

Solution

The man in khaki lied when he said Al "put
a big red lobster into the pan." Lobsters turn red
only after they've been boiled, and Al would
not have boiled a lobster twice.

The Case of
the Manufacturer's
Clothes

The body of T. B. Dowd, a manufacturer of men's hats, was found by two students in his expensive sports car parked in secluded Meadowlark Lane.

"Dowd was a lefty," Inspector Winters told Dr. Haledjian the next day at headquarters. "He apparently committed suicide.

"The bullet entered his left temple. When found, he was leaning over the steering wheel, slightly to the right of center. The pistol was on the floor by the clutch pedal."

Haledjian nodded thoughtfully and continued to study the pile of clothing which Dowd had been wearing.

On the police table were a pair of shiny black shoes, navy stretch socks, a blue suit, black leather belt, monogrammed underwear and shirt, a conservative tie, and two handkerchiefs — one soiled and one still folded for the breast pocket.

The inspector went on.

"Besides these clothes and the gun, the only other object in the car was a briefcase. It contained his firm's latest promotion campaign.

"Dowd told his secretary he was driving to

Convention Hall to attend the men's wear trade fair. He left his office at one P.M. The coroner places the time of his death around two-thirty P.M.

"He's supposed to be happily married and a financial success," concluded the inspector. "So why suicide?"

"It wasn't suicide," corrected Haledjian.

"The killer shot Dowd somewhere else, then staged the suicide in the parked car. But he forgot one item that gave the business away!"

WHAT?

Solution

A manufacturer of men's hats, Dowd would never have gone to a men's wear convention hatless, and no hat was found in the car!

The Case of
the Missing Model

"Jane left the house at three o'clock yesterday for the doctor's office," said her father. "She never came home. Her valise is still upstairs in her room, fully packed."

"She had planned on a trip?" asked Haledjian.

"To Mexico. Jane's a fashion model. She was to take part in a big fashion show in Mexico tomorrow. Her appointment with the doctor was for a vaccination."

"Did she keep it?"

"Well, I don't rightly know what doctor she went to, but she must have seen one."

"How can you be sure of that?"

"Charles Motley says so. I mean, he overheard Jane make a remark to that effect. Charlie lives next door, and about five o'clock as he was returning from work, he saw Jane and a man arguing near the bus stop on Weaver street. The man gripped Jane's arm. She pulled away, protesting, 'Don't, Ramon, I've just been vaccinated there. Stop it, you're hurting me!'"

"Didn't Charlie assist her?"

The father shifted uncomfortably. "Jane broke off her engagement with Charlie last month. I suppose he was still brooding. He saw this man and Jane enter a car and drive off. He didn't think it important till he learned Jane had van-ished. Now he won't forgive himself for not helping her."

"Can Charlie describe the man with Jane?"

"A slight man with a waxed mustache. Wore a dark gray overcoat that fitted too tight. Charlie thinks he's seen the fellow with Jane before."

Haledjian pursed his lips and reached for the telephone. "Inspector Winters will want to have a long, long talk with Mr. Charlie Motley!"

WHY DID HALEDJIAN DOUBT THE EX-FIANCE'S STORY?

Solution

Charlie Motley's slip was in stating that Jane had been hurt when the man gripped her vaccinated arm.

A fashion model, who must often wear sleeveless creations, would never disfigure her arm with a vaccination mark. She would be vaccinated on the hip.

The Case of
the Mistaken Shot

Shortly after midnight Dr. Haledjian received a call from Brad Worth pleading for help. Worth said he had just shot a man.

Arriving ten minutes later at Worth's beach house, the sleuth found a man lying face down a few paces inside the door.

"He's dead — don't touch him!" exclaimed Worth. "I've called the police. It was a mistake. He's my friend, Bill Mills!"

"All right, what happened?" asked Haledjian.

"Yesterday," began Worth, "an old classmate of mine, Chet Henry, came to see me. Chet is deaf, but he can read lips from an amazing distance.

"Chet wrote out a report for me. It said that around noon yesterday he noticed two men standing with their hands in their pockets, looking at my house. They spoke in whispers, and Chet, thinking this rather strange, stopped and observed them.

"Reading their lips, Chet learned that they planned to rob me of the Picasso hanging there."

Haledjian asked, "Why didn't you call the police then?"

"I was skeptical," said Worth remorsefully. "But an hour ago I heard the door open. I challenged the intruder. I thought he was pulling a gun, so I shot him. When I turned on the lights, I-I saw it was poor Bill Mills!"

"Very sad," said Haledjian, giving the "corpse" a gentle kick. "Okay, you can get up now. It was a good try at fooling an old detective."

WHY DIDN'T HALEDJIAN BELIEVE THE STORY?

Solution

Worth said that Chet Henry was attracted to the men because they were whispering. But as Henry was deaf, he couldn't have told whether they were whispering or shouting.

The Case of
the Mona Lisa

Bertie Tilford, England's gift to the international get-rich-quick set, decanted Dr. Haledjian's best brandy and sniffed critically.

Haledjian prepared himself for the latest of Bertie's money-making schemes.

"It is true," began Bertie, "that in the past I have asked you for money for enterprises which — I shall confess it! — were not quite proper. But now I've a chance at something big — da Vinci's Mona Lisa!"

"I thought the painting is in Paris," said the sleuth.

"Ha! So does the world!" exclaimed Bertie. "You will remember it was stolen in 1911. The painting which the authorities recovered was really a forgery by the superb Japanese counterfeiter, Yakki Yakameko.

"The genuine Mona Lisa was hidden in Tokyo till a buyer was found. Now it is coming to Texas, rolled up in a bolt of finest silk and shipped unwittingly by one of Japan's most reputable mills.

"I would not be a party to any criminal venture," Bertie hastily assured the sleuth. "I have, however, a contact who guarantees me that he can intercept the silk shipment and recover the painting. He needs only $30,000 to bribe the ruffians who guard it. The French will pay a reward of $1,000,000 for its recovery, I'm positive.

"If you could advance me the $30,000, dear boy," concluded Bertie, "I can personally promise you half the reward!"

"You won't get thirty cents," snapped Haledjian.

HOW COME?

Solution

The real Mona Lisa could not be "rolled up in a bolt of the finest silk." It is painted on wood!

The Case of
the Murdered Vocalist

The day after Dr. Haledjian was asked to solve the murder of singer Joy April, the international recording star, he was visited by Miss April's gray-haired manager, Chuck Petri.

"Miss April kept a most interesting record hidden in her vanity table," said Haledjian, as the two men took seats in the library. "It was apparently her little secret. Did you know about it?"

"No," said Petri with a worried look.

"A detective found it in the false bottom of the vanity," said Haledjian. "The theory is that the killer was searching her apartment for it when she surprised him, and he stabbed her with a letter opener. Are you at all interested in it?"

"O-of course. Do you have it?" asked Petri.

"Yes, and I don't blame Miss April for keeping it hidden," said Haledjian. "It's not exactly for public consumption."

As the sleuth opened the middle drawer of his desk, he saw Petri put on his eyeglasses, a movement the manager made awkwardly because of the bandages on his thumb and forefinger.

"Ah," said Haledjian, lifting out a leatherbound diary. "Miss April started it May 12. The last entry is the day of her death. She put down everything that happened in her life during those months, and you don't come off very well!"

"You can bet everything about me are lies," snarled Petri. "I hated her, all right. But I didn't kill her!"

"Perhaps not," retorted Haledjian. "But you'll have a lot of explaining to do to convince the police."

HOW COME?

Solution

When Haledjian mentioned the "interesting record" kept by Joy April, the singer, Petri put on his eyeglasses — and fell into Haledjian's trap!

Had Petri really known nothing about the secret diary, as he claimed, the word "record" should have indicated something to be heard, not read!

The Case of
the Nature Lover

On the night of June 18, Matthew Reynolds, a Wall Street broker, was shot to death in his duplex apartment. The police immediately threw out a dragnet for Bill McKay, who had publicly sworn "to get" Reynolds.

"Reynolds testified against McKay when McKay was sentenced for income tax evasion. He recently finished serving a year in prison," Inspector Winters told Dr. Haledjian as the pair drove upstate ten days after the murder.

"Yesterday," continued the inspector, "a hiker came upon McKay camping out. McKay claims to have been there since his release from prison a month ago. He hadn't heard about Reynolds's death, he said.

"He gave himself up to the local authorities voluntarily," continued the inspector. "I asked Sheriff Patch to guide us to McKay's campsite."

The sheriff's car was waiting on the side of the highway. He led the way over the rutty back roads as far as the two cars could travel.

Proceeding on foot, they tramped for miles back into the green hills, arriving finally at a tent pitched on a grassy meadow.

"McKay claims he has lived in this tent on this meadow for a month," said the sheriff. "He could have too, for all anyone ever comes by this spot."

"The airtight alibi," said Haledjian, ducking into the tent.

Two metallic objects glinted on the green grass by McKay's cot.

"Rifle shells, the same caliber used in killing Reynolds," said Haledjian. "You can take us to McKay now, sheriff. He's going to need a new alibi!"

WHY?

Solution

McKay claimed he had lived in the tent for a month. Yet inside the tent the grass was still "green."

After a month under canvas, the grass inside the tent would have withered to brown.

The Case of
the New Year's Eve Murder

Mugsy Flynn scowled at Inspector Winters and Dr. Haledjian. "You got nothin' on me," he snarled. "I hated Dee Dee McGhie, but I didn't bump him off New Year's Eve."

The inspector calmly met Mugsy's belligerent gaze. "We have a doorman who is pretty sure it was you who stepped from behind a parked car on Fifty-third Street and shot Dee Dee at five minutes before midnight."

"I was in a nightclub till after midnight!" bawled Mugsy. "I didn't come outside till everybody was huggin' and shoutin' 'Happy New Year!'"

"What made you leave just when the fun was really getting started?" demanded the inspector suspiciously.

"The dance band. They whooped up some rock 'n roll bit as the clock struck twelve. So I got up and left. That kinda music reminds me of my wife. Anyway, I hit the street and I remember lookin' at my watch — a minute after midnight. I saw a crowd collectin' —"

"What club did you leave?"

"How should I know? The street is full of joints. I guess maybe I was in half a dozen between ten and midnight. Say, come to think of it, I bet it was the Blue Door I was in."

"The bartender at the Blue Door remembers seeing Mugsy, but he can't be sure of the exact time," the inspector said to Haledjian after Mugsy was ushered from the office.

"You won't need the bartender's testimony if you can get Mugsy to sign the remarks he just made," answered the sleuth. "His own words destroy his alibi."

WHAT WORDS?

Solution

Mugsy claimed the band "whooped up some rock 'n roll bit as the clock struck twelve," in order to prove he was inside and not on the street when Dee Dee was killed. To Mugsy's sorrow, there is only one song played across America at midnight on New Year's Eve, and it's not rock 'n roll. It's "Auld Lang Syne."

The Case of

the Old-Fashioned Pen

Rodney Stites, professor of French at State University, lay slumped across his desk, an apparent suicide.

"I heard the shot about an hour ago," said Carl, the manservant. "I rushed in and called you right away."

Dr. Haledjian walked to the desk, situated in the middle of the professor's library. "Touch anything?"

"Nothing except the telephone," was the reply.

Haledjian examined the body. Death, which occurred within the hour, was due to a bullet fired into the right temple at extremely close range.

A thirty-two caliber pistol lay on the thick carpet to the right of the professor's head. On the desk was a note. Written in ink, with several splotches, it read: "I can't go on without Elsie."

"Elsie, his wife, ran off with a young artist last year," Haledjian mused.

He turned his attention to the old-fashioned quill pen clutched in the deceased's right hand. An open, antique inkwell stood next to the desk phone an inch from the pen point.

On the stand of the inkwell was engraved:

"For Rodney on our Tenth Anniversary. Love Elsie."

"Call the police," Haledjian told Carl. "The suicide note has to be a fake. This is clearly a case of murder!"

HOW COME?

Solution

held the pen.

the gun into his right temple. His right hand still

death scene. The professor could not have fired

The murderer blundered in arranging the

The Case of
the Overheard Gunshot

"I'm having trouble with Clara's — "

Dr. Haledjian heard Ted Felton's frantic voice at the other end of the telephone terminated by the sound of a gunshot.

Hurrying to Felton's bachelor apartment, he found the door unlocked. Felton lay on his stomach in the dining area, a yard from the dangling telephone receiver.

He had been shot from behind. The bullet had entered below the shoulder blade and emerged, Haledjian saw upon turning the body on its back, at the left breast.

Blood stained Felton's white silk shirt around the bullet's points of entry and exit. The only other blood was a small stain on the floor, and it was made all but invisible by the red carpet.

As Haledjian began a search for the bullet, he heard a gasp. A blonde girl stood in the doorway, her eyes wide. Haledjian introduced himself and explained his presence.

"I'm Clara Blakeless, Ted's fiancee," she said falteringly. "W-who did it?"

"Have you an idea?" Haledjian parried.

"Ernie Matte," replied Clara vindictively. "He's been mad with jealousy since I broke my engagement to him last month."

"Did he ever threaten Ted?"

"I don't know. But he threatened me. It would

be like him to shoot Ted in the back. He's such a coward!"

"Ernie Matte may be a coward," said Haledjian. "But I doubt that he shot Ted."

HOW COME?

Solution

Haledjian suspected Clara, who knew Ted Felton had been shot in the back.

Since the corpse lay on its back, she should have assumed, had she been innocent, that the blood-stained wound on the left breast was the bullet's point of entry and not its exit.

The Case of
the Parked Car

The waiter touched a match to Dr. Haledjian's order of Cherries Jubilee. Instantly, a blue flame sprouted from the dish.

"Puts me in mind of poor Walt Dahlgren," said Haledjian soberly.

"The movie magnate who took his own life last week?" inquired Octavia, his fair dinner companion.

"The manner of Dahlgren's death is still unsettled," pointed out Haledjian. "I'll tell you the important facts and let you be the detective.

"Dahlgren was found behind the wheel of his sedan. The car was parked on the grass of the Grenwich Parkway just below the Stillford exit.

"Death was due to a thirty-two caliber bullet which had entered at the right temple. A single-shot, thirty-two pistol lay near the accelerator pedal.

"The sedan was spotless, inside and out. A careful search — by vacuum cleaners — of the ground within twenty feet of the parked car disclosed only two apple cores, a stub of a week-old theater ticket, and a rusted earring.

"Dahlgren's were the only fingerprints found on the pistol. An autospy showed powder burns at the wound area and fresh cherries in his mouth and digestive system. He must have been eating the fruit up to the instant of his death.

"Now," concluded Haledjian. "Can you tell me why I think Dahlgren was not a suicide, but had been killed elsewhere and brought to the spot where he was found?"

OCTAVIA COULDN'T. CAN YOU?

Solution

Dahlgren had been eating fresh cherries "up to the instant of death." Yet the interior of the car was "spotless," and the ground about failed to disclose what should have been there.

Cherry pits.

The Case of
the Phony Cop

"I represent Franklin D. Van Clausand II," said Godwin, the attorney, settling himself in Dr. Haledjian's study. "The young man is being framed for robbery and murder. I'm hopeful you can clear him.

"Franklin has been working for a year in one of his father's banks," continued the attorney. "Last Tuesday, before the doors opened, a man dressed as a police officer gained admission. He looked like a motorcycle cop — black leather jacket, boots, sun goggles, and white crash helmet. He even had a badge.

"Franklin was closing the vault when the phony cop drew a pistol. Putting the muzzle against Franklin's neck, he forced him to fill a sack with bills of high denomination.

"As the thief was leaving, a guard drew his gun. Two shots were fired. The guard fell, dying.

"Franklin was able to provide the only description of the killer. An alarm went out for a man about thirty years old, six feet tall, with fair complexion, blue eyes, and a crescent scar on his upper lip.

"That afternoon one Edgar Burgess was picked up over in Flint for speeding. He answered the description. And $300,000 was found in his car.

"When informed who had given out his description, Burgress grew furious. He tried to implicate young Franklin, insisting he was a partner in the crime."

The attorney paused. "Franklin swears he's never seen Burgess except once — in the bank. But he's come under a cloud of suspicion."

"And there he must stay," said Haledjian. "He was obviously an accomplice, but lost his nerve when Burgess killed the guard."

WHY?

Solution

Franklin's description of Burgress was too good. As the "cop," Burgess wore sun goggles. Franklin could not have known his eyes were "blue" unless he had seen him before.

The Case of
the Phony Crash

Dr. Haledjian had just turned over drowsily in his sleeping bag when he saw a big car come down the short dirt road, which fed off the highway, and disappear over the cliff.

Running after the car was a tall man. He stopped at the edge of the cliff, lay down on the ground, and began to moan and shout, "Help! Help! My back!"

Four other campers reached the man before the thoughtful sleuth.

Haledjian bypassed the group and descended to the car.

It was overturned and almost totally wrecked. About the only things intact were the four worn-out tires, which still spun lazily.

Two days later Haledjian received Abbot, the insurance agent, who stated his difficulties.

"Starnes claims he fell asleep at the wheel and woke up just in time to escape going over the cliff with the car.

"At first we thought he needed money in a hurry and wanted to collect his auto insurance. The car is only five days old and worth $6,500.

"It turns out he's claiming he can't work a lick — hurt his back. You know about injuries there. He has a big monthly income policy, and we think he's shamming.

"You're the only witness," concluded Abbot.

"But Starnes's attorney will capitalize on the facts that it was night and you were barely awake, and therefore you didn't see clearly."

"You won't need my testimony," said Haledjian. "Starnes planned to wreck the car. That is obvious."

HOW COME?

Solution

Starnes, like many who fake accidents, had removed the new tires from his "five-day-old" car and replaced them with "worn-out" ones.

The Case of
the Poisoned Drink

"We're holding Eddie Jordon on suspicion of murder," Inspector Winters told Dr. Haledjian. "Yesterday Jordon and Harry Lewis ate lunch together at a crowded restaurant. When and how Jordon slipped the poison into Lewis's drink in front of all those people is a mystery.

"Both men ordered club sandwiches and soft drinks," continued the inspector. "Just as the waiter brought the drinks, Lewis was summoned to the telephone. The receptionist says that Lewis complained to her that he'd picked up a dead line."

"You believe that the call was a decoy to allow Jordon a chance to poison the drink?" asked Haledjian.

"So it seems. We know the drinks were all right when they were brought to the table. The waiter admits it."

"Admits?"

"The waiter says Lewis ordered a root beer and Jordon a sarsaparilla. He placed the order in the kitchen, and when he returned to pick up the drinks, he didn't know which was which. The chef didn't remember either.

"In glasses, the two drinks look alike," went on the inspector. "The waiter admits he sipped one to find out which was which. He tasted the root beer, which Lewis ordered. That means the root beer wasn't poisoned till afterward, or the waiter would have been poisoned too."

"A kitchen is a busy place," said Haledjian. "It was easy for the waiter to slip the poison into the drink he served Lewis."

The inspector looked startled. "But — why?"

"Undoubtedly because somebody — perhaps Jordon — paid him well. You won't have any trouble. The waiter will confess once you confront him with his lie."

WHAT WAS THE WAITER'S LIE?

Solution

The waiter claimed he established which drink should be served to Lewis and which to Jordon by sipping one — the root beer. However, it is impossible to distinguish root beer from sarsaparilla by taste.

The Case of
the Pudgy Playboy

It was the steadfast ambition of American toothpaste model Betti Allen, "the girl with the million-dollar smile," to acquire a corner of the wealth of Far Eastern playboy Abka Fazl.

Ungraciously, the pudgy Fazl was more bewitched by food than amour. So Betti was compelled to rest her charms and exercise her wits.

Over a table creaking with silver serving dishes the determined adventuress stared darkly as Fazl shoveled in crab meat ravigotte.

At eight-thirty P.M. a waiter entered the suite and served the dessert — blueberry pie surmounted by avocado sherbert — and coffee.

Fazl gulped nearly all the dessert before mouthing a massive belch. Eyes rolling, he toppled off the chair.

Fifteen minutes later Betti's urgent call for a doctor fetched Dr. Haledjian, a guest at the hotel.

Betti admitted him to Fazl's suite. She was able to smile bravely, a flexion which not only demonstrated her wonderful pluck but also displayed her dazzling white teeth to full advantage. She opened her baby blue eyes wide and pointed.

Fazl lay on his back, burping drowsily.

Haledjian reported the episode to the police. "The piece of pie left on Fazl's plate contained knockout drops. Miss Allen said she ate all of hers before passing out, and so a test was impossible.

"What about Fazl's jewels, stolen while the pair were unconscious?" asked the chief of police.

"That's a question for Miss Allen," replied Haledjian. "She was unquestionably in on the robbery."

HOW DID HALEDJIAN KNOW?

Solution

Haledjian knew Betti Allen had not eaten the drugged blueberry pie, and therefore she was conscious during the robbery. If she had eaten it, her teeth "fifteen minutes later" would not have been "dazzling white."

They would have been stained blue from the berries.

The Case of
the Railroad Crash

On the night of July 15, the engineer of a westbound local missed a signal and crashed head-on into the Rocket, a high-speed express out of Chicago.

The result — one of the bloodiest disasters in railroad history.

"It strikes me odd that all the serious casualties were in the first seven cars of both trains," said Dr. Haledjian. "All except one."

"Jess Fromm, you mean?" asked Inspector Winters. "What makes you question his death?"

"Partly because Fromm's niece asked me to investigate," replied Haledjian.

The inspector went to his files. "Fromm was on his way to a hardware convention with his business partner, Wendel Smith," said the inspector. "Here's Smith's statement.

"According to Smith, he and Fromm shared compartment C in the last car of the local. Seconds before the crash, Fromm got up and walked forward to the compartment's toilet.

"At the impact, Fromm was standing. He was thrown back and struck his head against the ridge of the card table set between the facing seats.

"Smith now owns the whole business," said the inspector. "There's your motive. Method? He could have struck Fromm in the back of the neck with the table AFTER the crash. But how are you going to prove it?"

"I should start," replied Haledjian, "with the obvious lie in Smith's statement."

WHAT WAS SMITH'S LIE?

Solution

Smith lied when he stated Fromm was "thrown back" at the impact.

Anyone standing, or sitting, in a speeding vehicle involved in a head-on crash is thrown forward at the instant of impact.

The Case of
the Shot in the Back

On a shivery November evening Dr. Haledjian was taking a constitutional when he heard a shot. He saw an elderly man suddenly lurch against the front door of a nearby house, fall, and lie motionless on the porch.

The two other men on the block joined the famous sleuth in sprinting to the prostrate man.

They found him dead, shot through the back.

After introducing himself, Haledjian snapped, "Each of you better have an alibi. I'm sure one of you shot him and tossed the gun away. But the police will find it."

Both men, who were wearing gloves and tight overcoats insisted they did not know the deceased. Each claimed he was simply taking the evening air.

"I'm Ted Baggs," said the first man. "I noticed the dead man locking the front door a split second before I heard the shot. I ran right up to him."

"I'm Sid Cole," said the second man, who had reached the porch last. "I heard the shot, but I didn't know what happened till I saw you two running for the house."

The key was still in the front door. Haledjian turned it, entered the house, and called the police.

"The dead man's wife is an invalid," Haledjian told Inspector Winters twenty-five minutes later. "She says her husband was going out to the drugstore. He habitually locks the house when he leaves her alone."

"Any leads?" asked the inspector.

"Yes," declared Haledjian. "Arrest —"

WHOM?

Solution

Ted Baggs — who knew Trill was locking (not unlocking) his front door.

Baggs must have been watching the house for a long time, otherwise he could not have known whether Trill was entering or leaving.

The Case of
the Silver Bowl

"I can't be certain from a photograph, but that looks like the gunman," said Fitzpatrick.

"Nose Cole," said Inspector Winters, glancing at the police album. "Two convictions for armed robbery. You say Cole entered the store just as it opened for the day?"

"That's right," replied Fitzpatrick. "I had my back to the door when I heard him enter. 'Don't turn around,' he commanded. 'I've got a gun, and I'll use it if I have to!'"

"Then what happened?"

"I did exactly as he told me. I passed all the silver to him from the wall showcase. I guess he put it into the bag I saw him carrying when he raced out the door."

"You saw his back," said Haledjian. "Did you ever see his face?"

"No. He made me pass each piece of silverware to him behind my back."

"Yet you claim to know what he looks like," interposed the inspector.

Fitzpatrick stiffened. "I saw his reflection. W-we keep the silver highly polished. As I passed him a large fruit bowl, I could see his image reflected on the inside of it. I saw him only for a few seconds. Maybe it wasn't Cole —"

"You seemed to be fairly certain a minute ago," snapped the inspector.

"Did you see the gun in the reflection?" Haledjian put in.

"Come to think of it, I didn't," admitted Fitzpatrick.

"You didn't see Cole, either. I suggest you return the silver you stole rather than continue this farce," admonished Haledjian. "It will go easier with you."

WHAT WAS FITZPATRICK'S BLUNDER?

Solution

Fitzpatrick could never have made an identification of a gunman or anyone else on the basis of an image reflected briefly on the inside of a polished bowl.

The inside of a bowl reflects images upside down.

The Case of
the Silver Pen

"The police were here all morning, dar-rrhhhling! It's been simply frightful!"

Covering her face with her delicately lotioned hands, Vivian Hobson, Broadway's brightest — if oldest — ingenue, slumped onto a purple chaise longue.

Dr. Haledjian, an old friend, studied the bedroom, from which the actress's daughter Shari had been kidnapped the previous night.

A rope fashioned of bedsheets and blankets and anchored to one bed leg dangled from the window. It reached to within a yard of the ground some dozen feet below.

"The kidnapper must have sneaked into the house during the day, because everything is locked at night," said Vivian. "I was on the balcony around midnight when I saw a man work down the sheets. He had poor Shari across one shoulder, limp. He must have knocked her unconscious, the ruffian!"

"Has anything been moved in the room?" asked Haledjian.

"No, everything is precisely as it was."

Haledjian walked outside. On the street he found a newsboy and gave him half a dollar to retrace the kidnapper's route down the bedding.

As the lad swung out the window, the bed

113

was dragged a few inches from its position against the wall, revealing a glittering object on the floor.

Haledjian bent over and picked up a silver fountain pen.

"Is it a clue?" exclaimed Vivian.

"Yes — a clue to a faked kidnapping," retorted Haledjian. "Your new play, 'The Kidnapped Daughter,' needs a bit of publicity. That's why you staged this, isn't it?"

HOW DID HALEDJIAN KNOW?

Solution

Had there really been a kidnapping, the double load of kidnapper and girl pulling on the bedclothes would have dragged the bed away from the wall, as the weight of the newsboy did.

The Case of
the Spinning Eggs

The soda fountain was deserted except for Dr. Haledjian and a red-headed youngster engrossed in spinning an egg.

Suddenly the egg twirled off the counter and dropped out of Haledjian's sight. There was a small crash, and the boy's grin turned to a look of dismay.

The counterman, to whom broken eggs were a regular occurrence, passed him a dustpan and broom.

At this point Haledjian paid for his sundae and departed. The incident was forgotten until that evening, when it was recalled by a visit from two boys in quest of a detective.

"We spin eggs," explained Glenn Stewart. "Whoever egg spins the longest wins."

"Red Mason's won everything. Bikes, skates, footballs. He never loses," moaned Larry Appleson. "You've just got to help us discover how he does it!"

"You suspect foul play?" asked Haledjian, frowning. "Suppose you tell me where the eggs come from."

"We get them fresh from the farm," said Glenn. "Each boy chooses his egg and lets his opponent mark it with a pencil. On the day of the match, the eggs are examined. That way we can tell if it's the same egg, and if it's been doctored up."

"A difficult case," muttered Haledjian.

The next afternoon he witnessed an egg-spinning contest. The champion, Red Mason, turned out to be the boy he had seen practicing on the drugstore counter.

Red's egg easily spun the longest. Grinning smugly, he walked off with his opponent's baseball glove.

"That will be his last victory," Haledjian announced. "I've cracked this case!"

HOW?

Solution

The fact that the counterman had handed Red a broom instead of a mop or towel with which to clean up the broken egg had tipped Haledjian that Red's egg was hardboiled. And a hardboiled egg will outspin a raw egg every time.

The Case of
the Stolen Pesos

Motoring through South America, Dr. Haledjian arrived in a mountain village as the local police were preparing to hang a man named Manuel Rodriguez.

The chief of police recognized Haledjian and promptly delayed the execution while he told the famous criminologist all about the case.

The previous month, said the chief, the national mint had been robbed of a million one-peso notes by a pair of masked men.

Three nights ago, Pedro Gonzales, a farmer, noticed a dim light in the window of an abandoned house near the village. Investigating, he saw two men seated by a candle, apparently arguing.

Pedro stopped outside of earshot, fearing to move too close. But he recognized one of the pair, Manuel Rodriguez, who had recently rented a room in his house. The next night, after Rodriguez went out, Pedro entered his room and found a new peso. Its serial number identified it as one of the stolen million.

Pedro immediately hurried to the abandoned house. This time he crept close enough to hear.

Rodriguez was in a temper. He insisted he had carefully counted his share again that afternoon and it wasn't half the loot — it was a thousand pesos short. The two men fought, and suddenly Rodriguez stabbed the other.

"I'm pretending to hang Rodriguez," whispered the police chief. "I want to scare him into telling me where he hid the million and the body of his partner."

"He can't tell you either," said Haledjian. "He's innocent. Pedro is trying to frame him."

HOW DID HALEDJIAN KNOW?

Solution

Pedro's mistake was in declaring that Rodriguez said he had "carefully counted his share again that day." Impossible!

It would have taken Rodriguez at least five days — working around the clock — to count "half the loot," half of one million pesos!

The Case of
the Stranded Blonde

A look of satisfaction settled on young Harrington's face as he sat at dinner with Dr. Haledjian.

"Last week I put to good use my long association with you, Doctor." The handsome youth puffed a moment on his cigar. Then he related what had happened to him.

"I was driving my convertible up to Albany when night overtook me, still fifty miles from my destination. I thought I'd better double check my route, and so I inquired at a roadside tavern.

"While I was endeavoring to catch the bartender's eye, an extraordinarily beautiful woman sat down on the stool next to mine.

"She begged my forgiveness for speaking, and, quite covered with embarrassment, confessed she had left her purse on the bus. What could I do?

"After three rounds of martinis, she refused another drink, but demurely asked for a quarter for the bus home. 'Nonsense!' I protested and escorted her to my car.

"We had driven but a mile when a pair of headlights swung into the road behind me. The girl turned around and uttered a cry. 'My husband! He'll kill us both!'

"The road being dark and unfamiliar, I de-

119

cided against a race. I pulled to the side and stopped. So did the black sedan following us. An enormous man jumped out, bellowing wrathfully. But I put an end to his posturing by pointing out the blunder in their plot. I drove off, leaving the pair of conspirators furious but far wiser."

"Congratulations," said Haledjian. "A simple case, but an instructive one. Henceforth you will be alert to the cunning behind a pretty face."

HOW DID HARRINGTON KNOW HE WAS BEING FRAMED?

Solution

It is impossible to identify a car at night while looking back into its headlights. The girl could recognize the car which followed them only if she knew beforehand that it would be there.

The Case of
the Stunned Nephew

Dr. Haledjian knelt down to examine the spider which had spun a beautiful, wheel-shaped web across the lower half the back door.

"A species of Argiopidae," said the sleuth.

"Uncle Phil would know its exact name," said young Bush. "He's sort of a bug himself. I-I mean he won't let me kill anything, even a rat. Look at his house — I can't even dust away the cobwebs for him."

"It's rather like a setting for a horror show," agreed Haledjian. "Suppose you tell me what happened here."

"Uncle Phil is in Europe on his sabbatical," began Bush, leading the way to the library. "He asked me to check the house once a week. I have the key to the front door.

"About an hour ago, I arrived to inspect the house. I heard noises as I entered.

"I called out. Suddenly a big man ran past me and out the back door. I might have caught him, but I tripped over a pile of bird food cartons in the hall, stunning myself.

"When I recovered, the intruder was gone. I found the safe as you see it, open and empty. I telephoned you right away from the house next door."

"What was in the safe?" asked Haledjian.

"I've no idea, but I can write Uncle Phil.

Here's his address," said Bush, producing a folded slip of paper.

Haledjian read: "Blue Lion Hotel, Harwick, Roxburgh, Scotland."

"Before you call the police," snapped the sleuth, "you had better improve your story!"

HOW COME?

Solution

Had an intruder escaped by the back door, as Bush claimed, he would have broken apart the beautiful spider web.

The Case of
the Suicide Note

"I heard the shot at about nine-thirty," said Mathews, the secretary. "I found Mr. Southworth in his den exactly as you see him."

The famous playwright and Broadway producer was dead of a bullet fired from close range into his left temple. His left hand clutched a thirty-eight revolver, his right held a pen with which he had apparently written the suicide note lying on the desk in front of him.

Leaning over the dead man's shoulder, Dr. Haledjian read:

"I no longer possess the health and strength to perform the labours which once brought me joy. I have received all the honours and riches any man has a right to expect in one lifetime. Now, before I become a burden to my daughter, Alice, I wish to depart this worldly theatre."

"Is this in Mr. Southworth's handwriting?" asked Haledjian.

"I'm not an expert, sir, but it does resemble his," replied Mathews.

"How many persons have keys to the house?"

"I do, sir, and the cook. Then there's Miss Alice, and Mr. Arnold."

"Who is he?"

"Mr. Arnold Southworth, a younger brother. He arrived from England for a visit and occupies the guest bedroom."

"Did the brothers ever quarrel?"

"On the contrary, they hit it off first rate. Mr. Arnold wanted Mr. Vernon to accompany him back to England this summer. When their parents were divorced, Mr. Arnold was reared in London by the father. Mr. Vernon remained with his mother in America."

"Did Vernon say he would go to England?"

"I don't believe he'd quite made up his mind. They discussed it again tonight, just before Mr. Arnold left for a dinner engagement."

"I shall be interested to hear Arnold's alibi for this evening," said Haledjian. "Vernon never wrote the suicide note."

HOW DID HALEDJIAN
REACH HIS CONCLUSION?

Solution

Three words in the note, "labour," "honours," and "theatre," reveal an invariable English spelling preference. Vernon, the American, would have written "labor," "honors," and "theater."

The Case of
the Uneasy Squirrel

The day after the Valley Park Bank had been robbed of $28,000 by three men, police arrested Phil Lott, a guard at the bank.

Lott had been under surveillance as the possible "inside man" in the robbery. He was caught with a bird house stuffed with $7,000, exactly a quarter of the loot.

"Lott insists he found the bird house by chance," Inspector Winters told Dr. Haledjian. "I want you to hear his story."

Lott was ushered into the inspector's office. After protesting his innocence, he repeated this story.

"Every day I eat my lunch at the park across the street from the bank," he began. "I always sit in the same secluded spot.

"I was feeding the pigeons when I noticed a squirrel on a tree, halfway between the ground and the lowest branch.

"Slowly, as if something in the branches made him uneasy, the squirrel backed down the trunk, reached the ground, turned, and scampered off.

"I walked to the tree, curious. Among the branches I saw a bird house which looked new to me. I climbed up and saw an oilcloth inside it.

"I took the bird house down to examine it.

That's when two men grabbed me. I never got my hand inside. But they found all that money in the oilcloth and arrested me. I'm innocent!"

After Lott had departed, the inspector said. "We're sure the money was Lott's payoff. But we can't crack that nutty story."

"Oh, yes, you can," replied Haledjian.

HOW?

Solution

Lott claimed that it was the curious action of the squirrel backing down the tree trunk that led to his discovery of the bird house. A lie!

Squirrels invariably descend a tree headfirst!